This book
belongs to:
_____

MADAME
Badobedah

For Jamie, Lyra and Margot: the adventurer crew.
With all my love — S. D.

For S .T. H. with love and art heists — L. O'H.

First published 2019 by Walker Books Ltd, 87 Vauxhall Walk, London SE11 5HJ

2 4 6 8 10 9 7 5 3 1

Text © 2019 Sophie Dahl • Illustrations © 2019 Lauren O'Hara
Hand lettering by Natalia O'Hara

The right of Sophie Dahl and Lauren O'Hara to be identified as author and illustrator respectively of this
work has been asserted by them in accordance with the Copyright, Designs and Patents Act 1988

This book has been typeset in Joanna

Printed in China

British Library Cataloguing in Publication Data:
a catalogue record for this book is available from the British Library

ISBN 978-1-4063-8440-6 (Trade edition)
ISBN 978-1-4063-9256-2 (Independents' exclusive edition (UK & Eire))

www.walker.co.uk

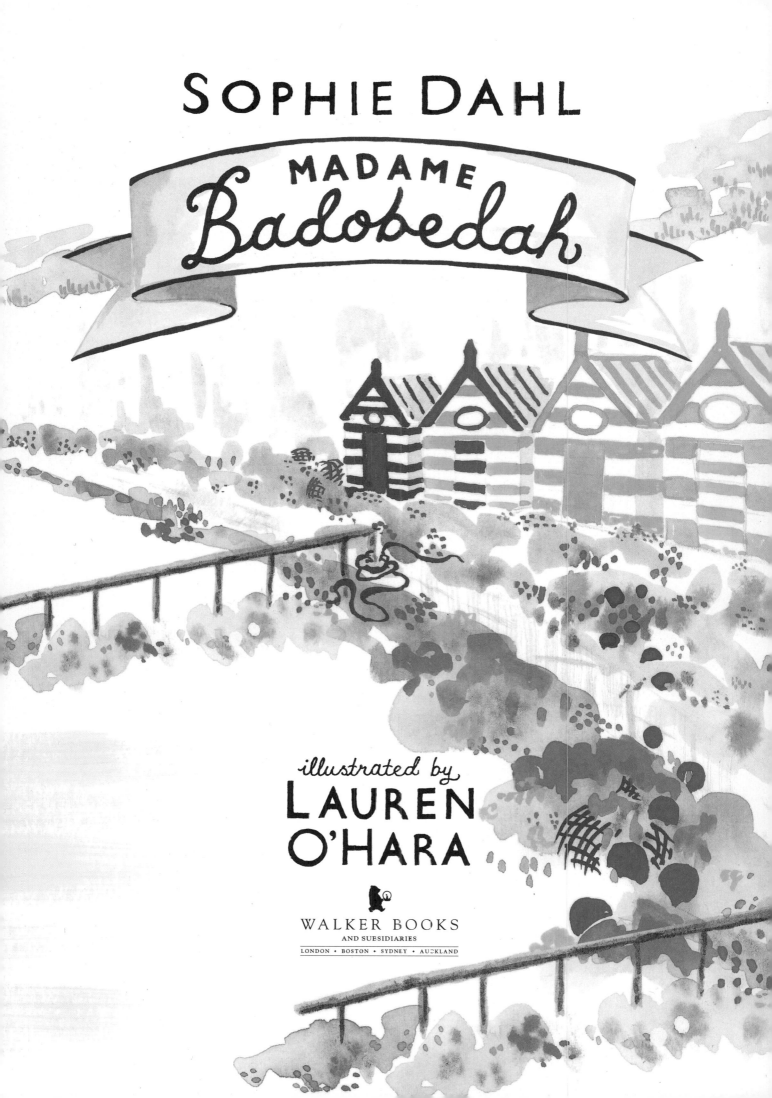

SOPHIE DAHL

MADAME Badobedah

illustrated by
LAUREN O'HARA

WALKER BOOKS
AND SUBSIDIARIES
LONDON · BOSTON · SYDNEY · AUCKLAND

Part One

The new (old) guest

My name is Mabel.

I live somewhere curious.

It's called The Mermaid Hotel.

My dad is the manager, but my mum is the BOSS.

Our back door leads to the sea, along a path of

old-men trees, battered and bent by the wind and salt.

Rock thyme twines with thistles

that spike your feet if you're barefoot.

But I don't care because I'm an adventurer.

And adventurers are often shoeless.

As well as
bare feet, adventurers
are keen on:

Swiss cheese,

the number eight,

donkeys

and Yorkshire puddings (I call them orchard puddings).

Adventurers DON'T like:

being told
what to do,

spiders,

ham

and plimsolls (because they smell like cardboard boxes).
Mine are too tight. They sit at school in a box with all the
other cardboardy plimsolls for company.

I am an only child. I can cross my eyes. And sometimes,
when I write, I get my ds and bs muddled up. My teacher,
Mrs Banks, says, "Mabel, your d is dancing to the beat of a b!"
And then she laughs. Bad joke.

I prefer home. No plimsolls; more bare feet. And adventure.
Lots of lovely adventure.

9

THE
Mermaid Hotel

Although The Mermaid Hotel is called a hotel, really it's a bed and breakfast.

This means you get a BED and BREAKFAST but you have to make your own lunch and tea.

The hotel has bothersome seagulls that shriek on the sills. And a mermaid over the front door, who I call Beryl In Peril because she's far from the sea, waving.

And inside: little packets of marmalade and butter that I hide in my pocket because they make a good snack.

But most importantly, The Mermaid Hotel has GUESTS: strangers that come and go. Some are delightful, some are like ham.

I am not a guest. I am a RESIDENT.

I'm going to tell you the story of our most interesting guest.

I was sitting under the front desk, minding my own business, when the bell rang. RIIIIIIIIIIIIIIIIIING!

I peered up.

She was old, old, old. With red lips.

She was not alone. She had:

two dogs,

two cats,

a tortoise

and twenty-three bags, all clustered around her like a choir.

I thought she might be a little bit awful.

"*Darlink*," she growled, "please remove yourself from under the desk and pass me my bag. The blue one there, to the right of that terrifically ugly coat stand. No, you frightful little child, not that one! Blue, I said!"

I passed her the bag. It felt like it had ten gold bars in it. I might have given her an icy glare. No one had ever called me such names before, and I'm keen on that coat stand.

The awful stranger didn't say thank you.

She trailed the smell of
old roses, spice and vanilla.
Her hair was red and crunchy;
a toffee apple without the stickiness. She wore
a cloud of feathers around her neck. Her head poked
out of them, like a cross ostrich pecking for grubs.

14

That was when I named her Madame Badobedah
(rhymes with *ooooh la la*). A good name for this growly-voiced,
suitcase-heavy, feather-clad guest – VILLAIN – that I was one
hundred and ten per cent sure she was.

Two big trunks, one dressing table, the twenty-three bags.
(Even the dogs had bags!)

Thirteen boxes and HUNDREDS of trinkets, all spilling
down the hall after her.

"Good grief, all this … this *stuff*!" my mum muttered,
as she and Dad staggered up the stairs. Madame Badobedah
walked silently behind, arrow-straight, carrying nothing but
a cushion with the tortoise balanced on it like a precious,
scaly emerald. She slipped a toffee in her mouth: she didn't
offer me one.

We stopped outside Room 32.

Room 32 has a bedroom and
a sitting room, one bath,
one loo, one sink, one
toaster and seven teacups but only four
saucers. Room 32 has an extraordinary
secret, too, but I'm not going to tell
you that now.

I know this because I know ALL
the rooms at The Mermaid Hotel,
along with their secrets. I don't have
brothers and sisters; I have rooms.
A room can be a lot like a person: it
sees stories and parties and bored days
and birthday cakes. And sometimes it
sees sad things, too.

So, with its secrets and saucers,
Room 32 now also had: Madame
Badobedah, two dogs, two cats, a
tortoise and *her* secrets. A whole heap
of them.

Room 32

"It was like a circus!" my mum said later. "Rude woman."

"Poor woman," my dad said. I wondered what he meant.

"Those TRUNKS!" Mum said.

I thought those trunks were brimful of stolen gold. That dressing table was spitting jewels. She's not on holiday, I thought: *oh, this one is NEVER leaving*.

I decided I'd better keep an eye out to see what that old sneak was up to.

"I'm just going upstairs to find a book!" I shouted.

"In a spy costume?" my dad asked.

"I'm wearing a raincoat and sunglasses because the weather forecast is varied," I said.

"Whatever you say, Mabel," Dad replied.

When a guest comes to stay, I'm not allowed to go into their room any more because it suddenly belongs to them and is *private*.

But it is, after all, where I live. A guest is just borrowing the room really. So sometimes I peep through the keyhole a bit, to see what's happening. Then I am not just Mabel, but Mabel The Spy.

And spies SPY.

To be the best spy, you need to be really good at observing people: what they are like, what habits they have. A habit is something that is hard to give up. I have the habit of biting my nails. Nails are so chewy and hard and delicious. I *might* also have the habit of picking my nose and wiping it on the wall.

And, after observing
Madame Badobedah through the keyhole for three
and a half whole minutes, I had a strong theory about her:
**SHE WAS, WITHOUT QUESTION, AN ANCIENT
SUPERVILLAIN ON THE RUN FROM THE POLICE.**
(Her chosen hideout: Room 32, The Mermaid Hotel.)

This was the evidence:

1. The fugitive looked around the room. She pulled out a pair of ballet shoes from one of the many trunks. She kissed them. Clearly she did ballet to get all limber for breaking and entering and for catapulting through museums in a catsuit.

2. A shopping list of strangeness exploded from her bags – a glimmering tiara, one ice skate, a Hawaiian lei and a pack of cards. Curious.

3. The fugitive hid a pile of
coins under her bed, in a sock. She
arranged the lei over it. She'd obviously
brought it to remind her of her family,
who were waiting for her in Honolulu.
She'd join them when the coast was clear.

4. A police car whistled past in the distance.
She sank down as though she was hiding.
And then the strangest thing happened:
Madame Badobedah sat on
the bed and cried.

I studied her for days. This is what I learned:

1. Madame Badobedah never went outside. Not ever.

2. No one knew her name. All the grown-ups called her
Mrs *mutter, mutter*. They seemed invisible to her. We all were.

3. That tortoise was the most suspicious creature I'd ever seen.
He had beady little eyes and he ran in the corridors like a
dizzy chicken. He ate bananas from her fingers, and bananas
are REVOLTING.

4. She did not say "darling" like anyone I knew. *Darlink*. It was pure menace, whispered like an insult.

5. She wore two pairs of socks on each foot. Underneath the socks, her toes were long and purple-ish with knobs on. They were grim. They were, in fact, the toes of a VILLAIN.

Since no one else seemed to care that we
were living with a high priestess of crime,
I realized I was on my own, as usual.
I would have to wait for the chance
to catch her red-handed.

Part Two

Sailing the high seas

One Saturday morning

I got in position again, stationed outside Room 32,

and sat patiently scratching a hole

in the carpet with my foot.

Spies are patient, you see.

This time – oh my days! – Madame Badobedah

opened the door. She seemed to know I was on the other side.

I pretended I was looking for a lost button.

"My favourite button," I said sadly, to the air. "Oh, where are you, dear button?"

Madame Badobedah said, "Would you like a cup of tea, darlink?"

"All right," I said. Even though I was a teeny bit scared. "But I'm not officially allowed tea. It wakes you up like billy-o, you know."

"Billy-o? What fun! Perhaps an unofficial sip? Your name is Mabel, isn't it?"

My heart was thudding. She knew my name! I followed her into Room 32. It felt different. It was bigger, cartoon-coloured; alive somehow.

The fire was roaring even though the sun outside was shining, and that shifty tortoise skittled along the floor like a man on a mission. Scratchy music played on a magic box.

Madame Badobedah's dressing table stood up against the wall as if it had always been there. Pots and cloudy puffs and lipsticks sat on top, in the shadow of a huge bottle of perfume that read: *Shalimar*. There were something like 507 drawers.

I wanted to know what was in those drawers. It itched inside of me. I asked her, like I didn't care, "So, what's in your drawers?"

"Diamonds, coins from Cleopatra's tomb, things like that," Madame Badobedah said. My heart did a swan dive. I wore my best spy face, where my eyes give nothing away.

"Hm," I said.

She poured me a cup of tea from a teapot wearing a jumper. "Even he feels the cold in this blasted country, poor *darlink*," she said.

The bed in Room 32 looked like a pirate ship. I decided it was time to put Madame Badobedah's villainy to the test.

"Do you know who Anne Bonny was?" I asked her.

"Questions, questions! No, why don't you tell me?" said Madame Badobedah.

"Anne was one of the most fearsome pirates of all time. She liked stealing gold. Probably kept it in socks." I stared into her eyes. I bet she had a picture of Anne Bonny in a frame somewhere with a heart around it.

"I'm a big fan of gold," Madame Badobedah replied smoothly. "She sounds marvellous. That bed of mine is a pirate ship – I call it the *Not-So-Jolly Roger*. Shall we set sail, Captain Mabel?"

I thought about it.

"Aye aye!" I said.
I heard the seagulls cry, and somewhere
in the distance a sea shanty echoed
through the mist.

The *Not-So-Jolly Roger* crew was weary after months at sea, the ship creaking with jewels, coins and exotic animals. There was a dodo in the dinghy, and a Cyclops-eyed parrot snored soundly on the cannon.

It was the first mate who spied the approaching storm, as she fed her cats anchovies. (Yuck, anchovies: spiny and disgusting.)

"There's a storm a-rollin' in, Captain Darlink!" the first mate hollered. "What is your command?"

"Stay calm, fellow!" I shouted. "Secure the animals safely in the hold! And for pity's sake, put the rubies in your bloomers!"

I steered the ship through
writing waves and slashing rain, past a
rainbow-coloured serpent and a school
of flying fish.

"I need a toffee too, sweets are vital in
a storm!" I bellowed as I saw that sneaky
first mate pop one in her mouth.

I navigated my trusty ship around
the treacherous rocks, leaning in as we
missed them by a breath. And as the
sun rose, we saw the green of land,
and the animals sighed with relief.
I straightened my hat as we docked.
The tortoise (whose name is Boris)
was a bit green around the gills
and wobbly on his feet.

It had been a successful voyage.

Then I remembered that while she might be
a good first mate, Madame Badobedah was
still a villain – most probably a *very* dangerous
criminal. Also, the room smelt of anchovies.
Time to escape. "Take care of your bloomers!"
I said, and ran downstairs.

Part Two (and a half)

Prehistoric bones and the excuses grown-ups make

All the grown-ups

said that Madame Badobedah was rude. My dad said she was rude because she was lonely. My mum said she thought she was a princess. I remembered her tiara.

Sometimes, before school I was allowed to take the Villain her toast and marmalade in bed.

"Come in, Captain Mabel!" Madame Badobedah would say, her voice a mixture of sea stones and honey all clanking together in a jar. She'd sit up in bed with a cough and a rattle. "A quick game of Old Maid before school? And *darlink*, could you open the curtains, please? I'm prehistoric and I don't think my bones have woken up yet."

If it was raining, which it did a lot, she'd say, "Oh well, I shall just stay in the pirate ship, ALL DAY." And she'd pull the covers up to her chin.

I think this was her big excuse to lurk inside all day, guarding her money sock. The weather is often used as an excuse by grown-ups.

Once, the phone rang and she picked it up and snapped, "No, I simply can't meet you at midday. I'm ludicrously busy." I held my breath. She snuggled back down into bed and winked at me.

Busyness is another well-known grown-up excuse.

But lying and avoiding people?

Hmm. SHADY LADY.

Part Three
The place where mermaids swim

When she was a girl,

before she was an international jewel thief ...

Madame Badobedah came from
across the sea on a big ship,
because there was a war.

She told me this as we drank hot chocolate on her bed. "When my ship docked in New York, I could still feel the ground moving under my feet for two whole weeks, even though I was on dry land. It was most strange!"

Madame Badobedah was a ballerina when she was young. She showed me how she could walk with a book on her head. The book perched on her nest of hair like a sparrow. "I was the Sugar Plum Fairy in *The Nutcracker!*" she said. "I wore a jewelled tiara. And once, I was so poor that I had to eat bread soup because the only thing in the cupboard was dry bread!" She laughed, spraying biscuit crumbs onto the cats and dogs.

She said a man she once knew always called her My Sweetheart. I think it was her husband, who is probably waiting for her in his shorts in the tropical breeze with the rest of her family.

She said a mountain of people asked for her hand. "But get that ring on your finger and he'll want the whole ARM, *darlink*! It's verrrrrrrry important for a woman to be independent, Captain Mabel. This you should know!"

I told her I could hold my breath underwater in the bath for forty-three seconds. This might be a lie.

"Because you're brilliant," Madame Badobedah said. "Can you ice skate?"

"No," I said.

"I used to love it, I'd skate on a river in the winter with my cousin Olga and we would swim in that very same river in the summer." Madame Badobedah poured me another cup. "Olga's eyes were the colour of shiny black beetles and she HATED saying sorry." She laughed. "It's so important in life to say sorry if one has gone wrong, *darlink*."

"Grown-ups never say sorry really," I answered. "But they expect children to do it all the time." I stroked Boris's scaly little foot.

"Well, Mabel, I want to say sorry to YOU," Madame Badobedah said. "I'm truly sorry I was grumpy and foul and said dreadful things to you when I first arrived. I was afraid of this new place and starting again. I'm so old to start again."

"It's OK," I said. I realized then that I really quite liked her. Even though she was on the run, with her funny habits and her toes and her banana-eating tortoise. Sneaky bird. I took a deep breath. "You don't even know the best secret about The Mermaid Hotel yet," I said. "It's in this room. It's even better than the pirate ship."

Madame Badobedah's eyes lit up.

"I'll take you. No one knows how to get there but me," I whispered, taking her soft, gnarled hand.

"I'm honoured," the Villain said. "I'm ready. Boiled sweet for the road, Captain?" She gave me a lemon barley sweet from the tin, all sneezy with powdered sugar. I pushed against the panelling on the wall, and a door opened.

"You thought it was just an extra cupboard!" I said, as we crawled in past the quiet and shushing dresses, and she laughed and said, "I did! Oof, my knees!"

"Are you all right, or do you need oiling?" I asked her.

"Oh, creaking is like laughing, my sweet. It means you're having fun," Madame Badobedah said. We slithered through a jungle of bags and shoes and I was pricked by a safety pin and we had to administer first aid with a tin box, some tissues and an old toffee.

"Being an adventurer can be dangerous," Madame Badobedah said. "But exactly the right kind of danger, *darlink*."

We had reached the end of the cupboard, where the last rafter met the ceiling. I knocked on it three times, and the mermaids answered me. They always do. They sang through the walls and their voices were sweet.

"The mermaids say you're a friend," I told Madame Badobedah, and she grinned, her teeth shining in the dark.

"I am," she said. I'd never seen her grin before.

"Shut your eyes and count to ten, please."

Madame Badobedah counted slowly.

"Now open."

Her eyes grew big.
"Oh Mabel, how wonderful!"
she said.

"Feel that balmy breeze! Look, there's the pirate ship, in the cove! And what's this? Oh, a waterfall! It's heaven. I'm so thrilled I brought my bathing costume!"

Madame Badobedah floated in the pool, drinking from a coconut, and the mermaids plaited my hair and told me they'd missed me.

"My cousin Olga would have adored it here," Madame Badobedah said, kicking her legs. "Simply adored it."

We were building a sandcastle and plotting a dive for pearls when I heard my mum call "MA-BEL!" up the stairs in her I Mean Business voice, and we had to tear ourselves away from paradise, crawling double quick back through the dresses.

I shouted, "I'm coming, Mum!" and that was when Madame Badobedah picked up something from her dresser and handed it to me. It was a huge, shimmering, real-life pearl. She closed my fingers around it and said, "A present. For you, adventurer."

I gasped. I wondered if it was from one of her heists. I don't know anyone else with precious jewels just hanging about. "Thank you," I said.

I didn't want to leave her. I wondered what she'd do when I was gone. She would sit by the window, I thought, with the dogs at her feet, and look out at the sea. She would say it was *achy-bones cold* and wrap a quilt around herself. Madame Badobedah says I have good bones and an old soul. She talks about bones a lot: old ones, good ones, cold ones, aching ones.

After my bath, I snuck up for a game of Old Maid on the pirate ship. We were both in our nighties. I wore my sunglasses so my eyes wouldn't give me away, and when I won, Madame Badobedah cried, "VILLAINESS!" and then she smiled, a great big smile, as big as the sky.

"But YOU are the villain!" I said. "Robber royalty." I took the sunglasses off. They had polka dots. Madame Badobedah has big green eyes with purple crinkles underneath.

"Gosh, am I?" she said. "A villain? My children certainly think I am." I didn't know she had children. They've never come to visit.

"You steal jewels and rob pyramids and are on the run with your animals," I said in a rush. "The Mermaid Hotel is your hideout. You'll be reunited with your husband one day on an island in the sun. I've worked it all out."

"Reunited?" There was a long pause.

She looked towards the sea, as she always did. Then she looked me dead in the eyes.

"Well, Captain, you've rumbled me, *darlink*," she said. "There's nowhere for me to run. Can we keep it between us? I'd like to live out my last days peacefully."

I thought about Madame Badobedah's lovely smile, how she always lets me be the captain, swims with mermaids, owns a tortoise called Boris and is never without a toffee. I thought about how she says sorry like she means it, has a perfume with a brave horse's name, *Shalimar*, and how she could pirouette through Cleopatra's tomb, arms full of treasure. I thought about pearls and bones and rainy days. I couldn't imagine anyone else would bring her toast and marmalade in prison. I'd be her only visitor.

"OK," I said finally, smiling at her. "It's a deal."

I'm going to sleep with Madame
Badobedah's pearl for the rest of my
life. I hid it under my pillow later,
stroking its cool roundness. I wondered
if I would dream of mermaids.

What does Madame Badobedah
dream of? Does she ice skate with
Olga, or sail the rocky seas towards
the island where her family waits?
And in those dreams, is she old or
is she a child?